The Mouse Who Wanted to Know

CURIOSITY'S STORY

ANNE MERRICK
Pictures by Tessa Richardson-Jones

Key to mouse
Parlours
1 Uppity
2 Homity and Dimity
3 Calamity
4 Alacrity
5 Serenity
6 Curiosity
7 Serendipity
8 Dignity
9 Oddity
→ → → → Tracks

Wild Wood

4

Harry's room

5

Kitchen
7

Cellar

9

Underground Spring

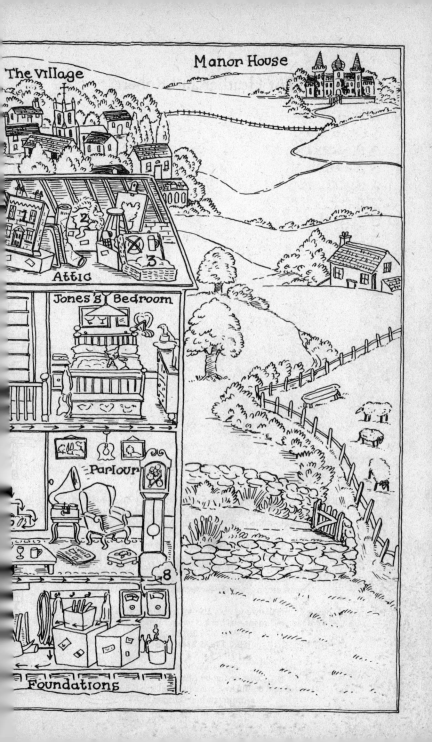

Manor House

The village

Attic

1

2

3

Jones's Bedroom

Parlour

8

Foundations

For Heather and Robert

First published in Great Britain in 1996
Text copyright © 1996 Anne Merrick
Illustrations © 1996 Tessa Richardson-Jones
The moral right of the author has been asserted
The moral right of the illustrator has been asserted

Bloomsbury Publishing PLC, 2 Soho Square, London W1V 6HB
A CIP catalogue record for this book is available from The British Library
ISBN 0 7475 2615 X pb
ISBN 0 7475 2641 9 hb
10 9 8 7 6 5 4 3 2 1
Text design by AB3
Cover design by Alison Withey
Printed and bound by Caladonian International Book
Manufacturing, Glasgow

In the space beneath the seventh stair of Mr and Mrs Jones's house lived a lively young mouse. Her fur was the colour of tree bark. Her eyes were like chips of black glass. And on the very top of her head there was a tuft of snow-white hair.

'Which shows everyone,' her mother told her, 'what a curiosity you are! Why – 'tis even shaped like a question mark!'

The seventh stair was exactly half way up and half way down the house so the mouse saw and heard almost everything that went on there. Light and air and an occasional crumb of food

drifted down to her through a crack in the floor-boards. And in Spring when the sun shone through the crack, it flashed on to the fragment of mirror that was propped in one corner and filled her whole Parlour with dancing light.

'I wonder,' said the mouse. 'How does it do that?'

In the mirror lived another young Mouse but it never answered her questions. Today as she spoke to it, however, she noticed something strange. When she opened her mouth the other Mouse opened her mouth too. She tried twirling her tail and at once the other Mouse twirled *her* tail. And when she waved one paw the other Mouse did the same.

'Are you ME?' she said to it. 'Is your name Curiosity?'

'Are you ME?' mimed the other mouse. 'Is your name Curiosity?'

'Curiouser and curiouser!' said Curiosity. And she did a little twizzle. Which the other one also did.

'That proves it,' said Curiosity, nodding her head at her other self. 'You have to be me!'

Beside the mirror there was a hole in the plaster. The hole opened into a secret passageway in

the wall and Curiosity peered out to see if one of her uncles or aunts or cousins were passing by so that she could call them into her Parlour and show them this marvel. She did not have to wait long before her cousin Uppity came scampering along the track. He was going so fast and looked so hot and bothered that Curiosity forgot she had something to tell him.

'Where are you going, Uppity?' she cried. 'What's happening? Why are you in such a hurry?'

Uppity scowled at her.

'Nowhere!' he snapped. 'And nothing. Mind your own business!'

The truth was he was running away from his Uncle Dignity who had threatened to box his ears for being cheeky.

'I only wanted to know, you know,' protested Curiosity as he brushed past her and scurried on down the track towards the kitchen. Turning back into her Parlour, Curiosity faced her other self in the mirror.

'Why is everyone always so cross?' she said.

It was true that the other Mice in the Mousehold were often impatient with Curiosity. Unless questions were to do with food or gossip, they did not want to ask or answer them. Wanting-to-know could lead to wanting-to-change and they were contented with things as they were. They thought they were very lucky to live in the Jones's house.

Mr and Mrs Jones were old – and growing older. They did not see or hear the Mice who shared the house with them. They kept no Cat and set no traps. Their kitchen was always warm, their larder was full of good things to eat and they dropped delicious tit-bits everywhere.

'What more d'you want, Man?' yawned Uncle Serenity when Curiosity complained to him that nothing exciting ever happened. 'Life's too short to worry. Take the World as it comes...'

'But,' said Curiosity to her other self in the mirror, 'this isn't the World, is it? This is only the Jones's house.'

Her own eyes looked thoughtfully back at her. And in them she thought she saw an answer.

CHAPTER TWO

Sometime later Curiosity left her Parlour and climbed the track to the Attic at the very top of the house. Patched with light and shadow the Attic stretched further than she could see. It was very quiet.

'Where is everyone?' she wondered.

Uppity, and most of the other up-and-coming young Mice, lived in the Attic. Although it was a long way from the kitchen where they went to forage, it was a good place to live. Sunshine

poured into it through the skylight and the wind sighed in under the eaves. And among the lumber that Mr and Mrs Jones had stored there over the years the Mice found safe and comfortable places to make their Parlours.

Best of all, through the gaps under the eaves, the Mice could see right across the Jones's garden and the Water Meadows to the Wild Wood on the rim of the World.

Curiosity gazed out at the World for a moment and then began to weave her way between boxes and cases and pieces of broken furniture until she came to The Doll's House where Uppity lived.

The Doll's House was shabby but still rather grand. The windows were curtained in gold brocade and the door opened straight on to a verandah where trees like round green lollipops stood in wooden tubs.

'Is anybody there?' called Curiosity as she climbed the steps to the verandah.

At one of the upstairs windows the curtains twitched and two heads appeared side by side.

'No,' said one of them. 'Nobody's here.'

'Don't be silly, Homity,' said Curiosity. '*You're* there!'

'He meanth Uppity'th not here,' lisped his

sister Dimity, cleaning one of her dainty pink ears. 'He'th gone to vithit Grandad. Can we give him a methage?'

'Well actually,' said Curiosity, 'I came to say goodbye.'

'Goodbye?' chorused Homity and Dimity. 'Whatever for?'

'Because I'm off to see the World.'

Dimity stopped washing her ears and Homity's eyes grew round as buttons.

'Oh dear!' he fretted. 'Are you sure? The World is so DANGEROUS!'

'Owl-th you know,' said Dimity. 'And CAT-TH!'

'Remember Grandad's stories,' Homity went on. 'All those dreadful things that happened to him...'

He trembled at the memory.

'What a *mouse* you are, Homity!' exclaimed Curiosity tossing her head.

Homity drew back behind the curtain and Dimity said gently, '*You* are a Mouthe too, Curiothity. And you're not a Field Mouthe, or a Wood Mouthe either. You are a *Houthe* Mouthe. Remember that.'

Then she too left the window.

Outside a black cloud began to nibble at the

sun and the light in the Attic went dim and grey.

'Quickety quick,' cried a voice behind Curiosity. 'Get a move on, slow coach!'

Curiosity turned around and saw her best friend Alacrity scurrying up the steps.

'Alacrity!' she cried. 'I wanted to see you. What d'you think about me go—?'

But Alacrity whisked round her and disappeared into The Doll's House. Curiosity wondered if she should follow her but it was getting late. And before she set out into the World she wanted to forage in the kitchen and say good-bye to Great-Great-Grandfather Serendipity.

'Ah well,' she sighed as she set off back the way she had come. 'I suppose Dimity will tell her...'

CHAPTER THREE

Except for the Parrot – who lived in a cage – the kitchen was deserted. Mr Jones was in the garden and Mrs Jones had taken the Dog for a walk. Even Uncle Serenity, who spent most of his time in the larder, was nowhere to be seen. Curiosity scurried to and fro across the floor gobbling up crumbs of toast and a shred or two of Weetabix.

'That's right, my hearty!' screeched the Parrot. 'Clear the decks!'

The Parrot had once belonged to a wicked seafaring man with a silver dagger and a wooden leg and she had travelled far and wide.

'I'm getting ready to go and see the World,' said Curiosity looking up at her. 'Where did you begin *your* travels?'

The Parrot clamped her beak around one of the bars of her cage.

'Madagascar,' she mumbled. 'Madagascar... Madagascar...'

The word came out blurred and Curiosity thought the Parrot was being rude. Flouncing away, she squeezed under the skirting board and went to say good-bye to Great-Great-Grandfather Serendipity.

'Mad to ask her!' she muttered as she slipped into his Parlour behind the stove. 'What cheek! I only wanted to know!'

Serendipity was curled up on the scrap of red velvet which once, long ago, his dear wife Charity had nibbled out of the Jones's curtains. While she waited for him to wake up Curiosity sniffed around his Parlour.

Because he was the oldest and largest and wisest of the Mice in the house, Great-Great-Grandfather had the best Parlour in the whole Mousehold. Fitting snugly into a cavity between two stones in the kitchen wall, it lay at the very heart of the house. In winter the stove kept it warm and in summer the breeze from the open door cooled it down. On the floor there was a patch of dried moss like a rust coloured rug. And above the place where he slept there was a ledge where he stored wedges of his favourite mouldy cheese and melty bits of chocolate.

Curiosity was just rearing up to examine this shelf when Great-Great-Grandfather woke up.

'My dear Child,' he said, rubbing his eyes and trying hard to remember which of his great great-granddaughters she was. 'How nice to see you!'

'I've come to say goodbye, Grandfather,' she said. 'I've decided I want to go out and see the World.'

Stiffly Serendipity stood up.

'My dear Child,' he murmured. 'Before

you rush away think hard and think well. The World is a most DANGEROUS place. If it isn't CATS it's OWLS. If it isn't FAMINE it's FLOOD. If it isn't STREETS it's DRAINS.'

He smoothed down the fur of his belly which was tipped with white as though frost had touched it.

'Many, many moons ago,' he said, 'your Great-Great-Grandmother Charity and I travelled through all the difficulties and dangers of the World until we found refuge here in the Jones's house...'

He paused. Inside his head he saw the cold white eye of the winter moon under which they had journeyed. He heard the bark of the fox and the swoop of the hawk...

Curiosity fidgeted about. She wanted to be off but Serendipity seemed lost in his thoughts and she did not like to leave before she had his blessing.

'Ah well,' he said dreamily. 'At least it's Spring again. And Spring – as our poet Jawser said – is the time when folk long to go on Pilgrimages!'

'What's a Pilgrimage?' asked Curiosity.

'My dear Child,' said Great-Great-Grandfather. 'A pilgrimage is a sort of Quest. And you are clearly a questioning, *questing* Mouse. What's more, although the World is Dangerous, it is also a Most Marvellous place...'

Raising his head he nudged a flake of chocolate off his shelf.

'Go off on your Quest with my blessing,' he said as he pushed it towards Curiosity. 'Find out about the World for yourself. You have your Great-Great-Grandmother's eyes. I know you will bring honour to our Tribe...'

CHAPTER FOUR

'Here we go... here we go... here we go...' trilled Curiosity as she scampered down the garden path.

The forests of grass on either side of her breathed out a wild, green-leafy smell that made her heart flutter with excitement.

'Grandfather is right,' she said. 'The World is Most Marvellous. Why didn't I do this moons and moons ago?'

A Starling strutting across the lawn stopped and looked at her in surprise.

'I don't know,' he said. 'What is it you're doing anyway?'

'Going on a Quest,' she said.

The Starling whistled and jabbed his sharp beak into the earth. Curiosity splashed through a puddle and because she'd never met a puddle before she turned around and splashed back again. Then, right there, in the middle of the path, she began to twizzle for joy.

Twizzling was something Curiosity had discovered she could do when she was no more than a few days old.

'Look, Ma!' she cried. 'Look at me!'

With her front paws stretched out for balance she reared up on her hind legs. Then lifting the right one she twirled slowly round on the left.

'What d'you call this, Ma?' she asked.

'I call it daft!' said her mother. 'Stop it at once! You'll addle what little brains you've got!'

But instead of stopping, Curiosity went on and on. She practised until she could spin so fast on her left hind leg that she became almost invisible.

'Groovy, Man!' laughed Uncle Serenity when he caught her practising in the larder one day. 'I really dig that stuff!'

He tried to stand on one leg himself. But he was so old and fat and top-heavy that he

toppled over and flopped head first into a dish of
Mrs Jones's strawberry jam.

'A Mouse ain't built to *twizzle* like
that!' he puffed as he climbed out,
spattering red juice everywhere. 'I don't

believe any other Mouse in the World could do such a thing. You were playing tricks with my eyes, Man!'

Now, as Curiosity twizzled on the path, it was as if the World itself played tricks with *her* eyes. The green of the grass, the gold of the sun and the blue of the sky all melted together into a shining hoop that whirled faster and faster about her while she stayed entranced and still at its centre.

She did not notice the clouds flocking together across the sky until water started to spit out of them. The drops were heavy and they hurt. She had never before felt the fall of rain.

'Stop it!' she said crossly as she slowed down.

But the rain did not stop. It dripped off her whiskers and dropped off her nose. It danced all round her on the path so that she could not see where she was going and it drummed so loudly in her ears that she could not hear *anything*.

'Now what?' she muttered as she staggered this way and that. 'Nobody warned me about RAIN!'

She bumped into the garden gate and crawled beneath it for shelter. On the other side a wide grey road wound away from her in both directions.

'Which way?' she wondered.

'To the Village,' said a signpost in the hedge pointing to the left.

'Thank you,' said Curiosity.

And as the sun escaped from the cloud, making the wetness on everything blaze and dazzle, she set off to find it.

CHAPTER FIVE

The way to The Village seemed long and dangerous. On the grass verge Curiosity struggled through a jungle of dandelions and daisies, while on the road beside her cars fumed along in a fury of smoke and glittering spray.

'Long, long ago,' said Great-Great-Grandfather's voice inside her head, 'I lived with my mother and father in a Tower built of glass. The tower was so tall that when it rained its roof was lost in the clouds. And when the sun shone

its walls shimmered with reflections of the City and the sky. But on the road at the foot of the tower CARS raced up and down, roaring and breathing out smoke, like Dragons...'

'Dirty, disgusting old Dragon!' cried Curiosity as a red car roared past, drenching her with water.

She was glad when the verge came to an end and she found herself on a stone path. Here the going was easy. Instead of fields there were now houses on either side of the road. Some of them crowded close together as if for company and some stood alone in their gardens like the Jones's house.

'Is this The Village?' she wondered.

She scurried along enjoying the wonder and strangeness of it all. From time to time there were

trails she wanted to investigate and side-tracks she wanted to take but now there was a new danger. People. As she went deeper into The Village their strong, salty smell was everywhere. Above her their voices quacked and growled and shrilled and gobbled. And beneath her she felt the earth quake and shiver as they trod it with their heavy feet.

The Feet were the worst thing. Soon Curiosity was having to scuttle this way and sidle that to save herself from being trampled.

'Help!' she squeaked as she dodged from under a huge black heel that was about to crush her.

'I'll be squashed as flat as one of Mr Jones's old socks!'

The People seemed to be busy with their own Quests and none of them saw Curiosity. She was wondering how long the street was going to go on when she darted between a pair of green Wellington boots and came face to face with a Dog.

Curiosity was used to the Jones's dog who did not believe in Mice. He never took the slightest notice of any of her Tribe even when they ran over his toes or tickled his nose. So she did not think to be afraid of this one.

31

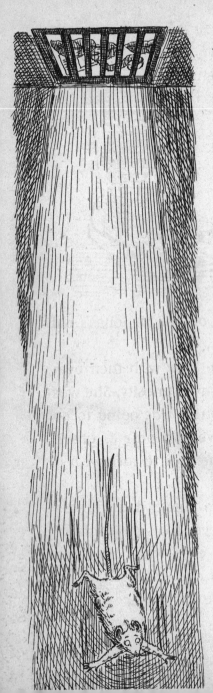

'Hi,' she said. 'Where is this path taking me? I'm going on a Quest and I need to…'

The Dog, who was dragging his Owner along on a leash, bounded towards her.

'What?' he barked. 'What? What?… What?'

His leash stretched across the path and tightened against the Wellington boots. The Boy in the boots tripped over it and went sprawling. The Owner fell over the Boy. And the Dog pranced in circles, tying his leash into knots and beating everyone with his feathery tail.

'I only wanted to know, you know!' squeaked Curiosity as the tail swept her right off the path.

The commotion went

on and on behind her as, curled into a ball, she bowled along the gutter. Then before she had time to gather her wits or get back on her feet, she rolled between two round, iron bars and fell into a funnel of darkness.

Down and down she plunged while the barred square of daylight through which she had dropped dwindled to a bright faraway spark.

'I wonder,' she moaned. 'Is this a chimney? Because if it is – and there's a fire in the hearth – I'll be frizzled to a cinder!'

CHAPTER SIX

At the bottom of the funnel there was not fire but water. Curiosity landed on a pile of rotting leaves which were so soft and squelchy that she sank deep into them. For a moment she lay there wondering if she were still alive or if she had fallen into the Land of Shadows. It was very dark, the air smelled sour, and she could hear the sound of running water.

After a while she clawed her way out of the heap and saw that she was on a narrow ledge. The ledge ran along the side of a tunnel that was as black as the Foundations of the Jones's house. The light from the distant grid flickered briefly on the surface of a stream as it slid past her and

from the tunnel roof drops of water plopped into it with a dull, dead sound.

'If it isn't streets,' said Great-Great-Grandfather's voice in her head again, 'it's DRAINS.'

'Is *that* where my Quest has brought me?' said Curiosity.

While she thought about this and about what to do next, she groomed her fur which was all gummed up with slime from the leaf pile. She was nearly clean when little ripples began to lap against the wall beneath her ledge and peering over she saw something floating towards her down the middle of the stream. As it drew closer, the light from the grid glinted off two dark squinty eyes. And below the eyes she could see a long snout pushing steadily through the water.

'Please, Sir,' cried Curiosity. 'Can you tell me

which is the quickest way to Outside? I want to know, you know, because I'm on a Quest and although I'm sure this drain is very interesting I'd really rather...'

But the creature showed no sign of having seen or heard her. Its eyes stayed fixed on the tunnel ahead and, paddling on, it soon vanished into the dark.

'The Rat!' exclaimed Curiosity. 'And after I was so polite too!'

She had never before met a Rat but she knew all about them from the stories told by her family.

'Snooty, stuck up critturs is Rats,' her mother always said. 'But treat 'em with respect and they'll leave you be.'

Curiosity tossed her head and decided to follow the Rat down stream. She had not gone far when she came across a damp packet with a few soggy crisps inside it. They tasted like wet cardboard but Curiosity was too hungry to care. As she chewed the last shaving of potato she heard water cascading down the funnel behind her.

'Now what's happening?' she cried.

Shuffling round she saw the stream froth and bubble as the waterfall splashed into it. Up in the street another shower of rain was falling and from all the gutters of The Village water was gushing into the drain. The water started to rise up the sides of the tunnel and huge waves came rolling towards Curiosity. The tunnel boomed as though somewhere a terrible Monster had broken loose.

The stream reared up over the ledge. It dragged at her paws and tugged at her tail. She tried to climb out of the way but the walls were

too smooth and slippery for her claws to grip. As she slithered back it snatched her up in its cold, soft jaws.

'Where are you taking me?' she squealed. 'Put me down!'

But gurgling with laughter the water whirled her round and carried her down into the bellowing darkness of the drain.

CHAPTER SEVEN

The stream soon grew bored with the game and settled down to a quiet steady flow.

'How did I learn to swim?' Curiosity asked it as her paws moved through it in a slow, pleasant rhythm. 'Who taught me?'

The water chuckled but did not answer. Soothed by its gentle rocking she was half asleep when in the blackness ahead of her she saw an O of daylight. The O grew rounder and larger and moments later she slid over the edge of something. Sunlight struck the water, splintering it into thousands of stars, as she dropped with a splash into yet another stream.

Curiosity drifted happily among the stars until she came to a stop among glossy leaves of cress and golden cups of marsh marigold. Nosing her way through the tangle of their stems she climbed out on to the bank of the brook and looked around her. She was surrounded by fields and The Village was nowhere to be seen.

'Where am I?' she asked a Robin who cocked one eye at her from his perch on a broken wall.

'Where are you? Where are you?' chirruped the Robin. Then matching his notes to the melody of the brook he sang her a song which charmed her but not answer her question.

Exploring about a bit, Curiosity found two violet flowers that tasted of honey and some tender shoots of winter wheat. She scrambled over a mountain of stones that had fallen out of the wall and made a long detour around an entanglement of blackberry bushes. She climbed in and out of several ditches.

'This Quest is full of interesting adventures,' she said to herself. 'But I don't think I want

to stay Outside for ever. It's too big...'

The sun slipped behind the high wall and she shivered, remembering Dimity's warning.

'You are not a Field Mouse or a Wood Mouse. You are a HOUSE Mouse. Remember that...'

Curiosity could see that it was not safe to remain where she was. Already the sky was turning pale with evening while above her a flock of Starlings swooped and swirled, searching for a place to roost for the night.

Wearily she followed the wall until it came to an end. And there, on the far side of a massive iron gate, she found a house.

The House was huge. It had towers and turrets and walls notched like battlements. Rows and rows of windows peeped like glassy eyes through the curtain of ivy which covered it. Its door was as wide as a church door and the steps which climbed up to it were guarded by stone lions. Across the lawns which lay between her and the House, hundreds of daffodils nodded their yellow heads at Curiosity.

'Here you are,' they seemed to say. 'This is it! This is where your Quest has brought you.'

Curiosity did a quick little twizzle of triumph and scampered under the gate.

As she waltzed across the velvety grass, she heard the warning clack of a magpie which flew out of the chestnut tree in the middle of the lawn.

'What's that about?' she said. 'It's only me!'

She did not notice the bushes against the house wall quiver and sway as something moved stealthily through them. She did not see the step where the lawn ended until she fell down it.

Picking herself up she started to cross the path

when, with a loud hiss and a snarl, a monstrous orange face came bristling down on her.

'Now what?' cried Curiosity, backing against the edge of the grass. 'Who on earth… ?'

Grinning a white and wicked grin the face rocked back and forth only a whisker's length from her own. The fur of the face was as fiery as the sun but out of it two green-gold eyes glared coldly as the moon. And as the curved white claws flashed out at her, Curiosity did not need an answer to her question. For she knew that this was the Creature which, since Time began, had stalked the nightmares – and the legends – of her Tribe.

CHAPTER EIGHT

The Cat menaced Curiosity with his grin and mesmerized her with his glare. An icy coldness crept from the tip of her tail to the tip of her nose. Her mind went blank and as though the blood were freezing in her veins she could not move.

The Cat reached out one paw and gave her a gentle blow. Then he waited with fangs bared until she stirred again and

struck harder with the other.

Dreamily Curiosity wondered how Uncle Serenity had escaped when the Stray Cat had wandered into the Jones's kitchen and caught him snoozing beside the stove. But her head was full of ache and she could not remember.

With his muzzle low to the ground and his haunches raised ready to spring, the Cat crouched on the path. He seemed to be very far away but she could feel his hot, fish-smelling breath on her face. She longed for sleep and her eyes were beginning to close when another of his buffets flipped her up in the air. She flopped down beside one of the stone lions at the foot of the steps and her eyes shot open with the shock. Between the stone and the ground she saw a thin, black slit.

'Is that a *hole?*' she said.

The question jolted her back to life. Paddling on the gravel with her paws she pushed herself towards the slit. Her whiskers prickled against its sides. Behind her she heard the spurt of pebbles as the Cat pounced. There was a sharp pain in her tail and, whisking it around her, she thrust deeper into the gap.

Chippings of stone and clods of earth

spattered over her as she scrunched herself tight into the tiny space. The Cat scratched furiously at the place where she had disappeared. But gleams of light seeping in around him showed Curiosity that his searching paw was never going to reach her.

Slowly her heart unfroze. Every bit of her smarted from the battering the Cat had given her. Scuffling about in the dry earth she managed to scoop out a hollow so that her back was no longer jammed against the stone above. Then she started to lick the blood from her injured tail.

The Cat stretched himself out on the path and

glowered in at her under the overhang of the rock. The pupils of his eyes were like two black holes rimmed with green fire.

'Don't thing you've got away,' he hissed. 'I've

waited many moons to catch one of *you!* I'm not going to give up now!'

'What d'you mean?' asked Curiosity, pricking up her ears. 'You haven't waited more than five twitches of your tail to catch ME! I've only just arrived. And by the way, where exactly am I? What is this place? Who lives in this House? And why... ?'

'Questions. Questions. Questions!' snarled the Cat. And resting his head on his paws he fell asleep without answering one of them.

CHAPTER NINE

Curiosity must have dozed off because the next thing she knew was that water was bubbling under the stone lion and trickling towards her through the dirt. Looking up she saw raindrops exploding on the ground outside the entrance to her hiding place. But she could not see the Cat.

'Scaredy Cat!' she jeered. 'Frightened of getting his fine orange coat wet!'

In case he was hiding close by, however, she crept out very cautiously. She was stiff from being squashed up and still sore from the Cat's blows. What with that and having to keep a look-out for him it took her a long time to climb the steps to the door of the house and it was dark by the time she reached it. Finding there was no gap beneath it she moved on to investigate the wall under the creeper.

Beneath the first window there was a place where the mortar had crumbled away between the stones, leaving a deep crevice in the wall. Curiosity wriggled into it.

'Just as I thought,' she said as the crack opened

up into a wide passageway. 'It's exactly like the Jones's house.'

But in the Jones's house she knew where every track led. Here, no matter how many turnings she tried, none of them seemed to lead anywhere except to another turning.

At last a wink of light showed her where there was a chink in the wall. Peeping through it she saw a room as big as the Jones's Attic. Like the Attic it was full of lumber, but everything was draped in white sheets so that in the moonlight the tables and chairs glimmered like shapeless ghosts of themselves. The windows were bare but on the walls there were curtains embroidered with pictures of Wolves and Bears lurking in the Wild Wood.

Curiosity cast about until she found a hole in the wall big enough to squeeze through. She was so tired that she simply slid down the back of one of the tapestries and dropped onto the crumpled sheet beneath it. Dust rose in a cloud around her as she sank into its softness and warmth. And before she could even wonder where she was, Curiosity was asleep.

She was woken by a rustling, whispering sound.

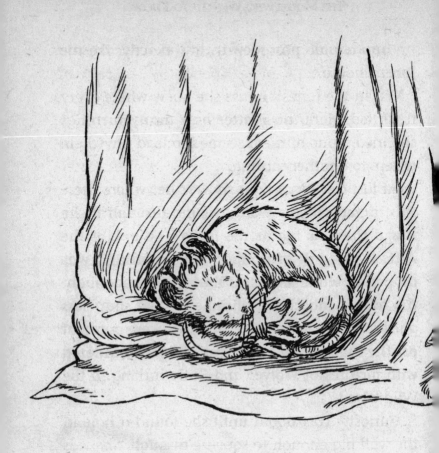

For a moment she stayed curled up with her eyes
fast shut, trying to remember where she was.

'Alors, mes amis,' said a voice. 'What 'ave we
'ere?'

The words were so strange Curiosity thought
she must have dreamed them. There were more
rustling sounds and dust smoked up from the
sheet. Somebody sneezed twice.

'A common-or-garden tramp, dear boy!' said another voice. 'A mere Nobody by the look of her!'

'Precisely!' fluted a third voice. 'Exactement!'

Curiosity opened one eye. Through the fog of dust she saw three faces staring at her. The faces were like her own – and yet not like. They were thinner and darker and their noses were very long.

'I am not a tramp,' she protested, standing up and facing them. 'And I am not a Nobody. I am a Mouse of the Tribe of Mousity.'

The three strangers looked down their long noses at her and two of them snorted with laughter.

'Who are *you*, anyway?' Curiosity demanded.

She did not take to these unfriendly Mice with their superior airs and haughty voices.

'Mon Dieu!' exclaimed the one who had first spoken. 'She 'ave the cheek to ask us oo we are! WE – oo 'ave lived in zis Manor 'Ouse since our ancestors came over 'ere...'

'Exactement,' agreed the high voiced one. 'In 1066 and all that. With William the Conker!'

The lips of all three curled over their pointed

front teeth and they stared more coldly than ever down their noses. Questions raced through Curiosity's head but before she could decide which one to ask, the largest one spoke again.

'I,' he said, 'am Bertrand Hubert Marmaduke de Souris. This is my brother Ralph. Pronounced RAIF of course. And this,' he added, scarcely glancing at the third Mouse, 'is our sister Amy.'

'Spelt A-I-M-E-E,' trilled Aimée. 'Meaning – of course – The One who Is Loved...'

Bertrand and Ralph both sniggered and Curiosity felt suddenly sorry for Aimée.

'Please,' she said to her. 'Is there anywhere I can forage? I haven't had a crumb since yesterday when a terrible orange Cat...'

The three de Souris backed away from her, their expressions changing from haughty to horrified.

'Mon Dieu!' said Ralph. 'She means ETHELRED!'

His eyes shifted this way and that as though he expected to see the Cat appear out of thin air and Aimée tried to burrow into the sheet beside Curiosity.

'I met him *Outside*,' explained Curiosity, hoping to calm them down. 'In the garden.'

Bertrand shuddered.

'Ethelred,' he groaned, 'is our Mortal Enemy!'

'E 'as us under siege,' said Ralph. 'We are trapped 'ere for ever in zis cold, droughty room...'

'*Draughty*, dear boy,' said Bertrand.

'Exact... ement,' quavered Aimée, emerging from the sheet.

Falling silent together they gnawed moodily at their tails. If her head had not already been in a whirl, Curiosity would have done a twizzle to cheer them up. But since they did not stir, she decided she would go and look for food herself.

As she set off across the floor her paws snagged on threadbare carpets and pattered over polished wood. Through the high Drawing Room windows she could see the bare branches of the Chestnut Tree, black against the blue sky. And climbing stealthily among them was the monstrous orange Cat.

Reaching a place where two floorboards had shrunk away from each other Curiosity sniffed at the gap. Faintly, from a long way off, she caught the crisp, hot smell of bread toasting.

'So there *are* People in this house!' she said.

CHAPTER TEN

While the hedges were unfurling their first green leaves and the sticky buds on the Chestnut Tree were swelling fit to burst, Curiosity went questing all over The Manor House. She scurried up staircases and skulked in sculleries. She lurked in the library and loitered in the laundry. She found the house was very grand but rather gloomy. And she was always hungry.

The People, who lived in the part of the building that Bertrand called the West Wing, were not a bit like Mr and Mrs Jones. They dropped very few tit-bits and they locked all their leftovers away in the fridge.

'If Mrs Jones lived here,' she said to the de Souris, 'there would be a larder – with yellow cheese and apple pie, gingerbread and chocolate cookies...'

'Oo are zese *Jones* you keep talking of?' said Ralph.

But when she started to explain he lost interest and scuttled back to his Parlour under the sofa. The de Souris were so scared of Ethelred that they hardly ever left their Parlours. They only came out to forage late at night when the Cat was locked out of the house and Curiosity began to see why they were so thin and miserable.

'Why don't you come exploring with me?' she asked Aimée one day. 'We could have a bit of fun! The Cat spends most of his time Outside. And when he's inside he's only in the West Wing!'

But Aimée twitched and shivered and a tear rolled slowly down her long nose.

'Sometimes,' she said, 'he escapes. That's how he killed our mother and father. And he caught our brothers and sisters when they were frolicking in the Ballroom!'

So, instead of going questing, Curiosity stayed in the Drawing Room and played Hide-and-Seek with Aimée.

When it was her turn to hide, she climbed up through the oak leaves and acorns carved on the fireplace and found herself on the wide, wooden mantel shelf above the hearth.

From this high place she could see the sunlight sparkling on the great glass chandelier that hung from the ceiling. And looking across the room she could see straight through the middle

window into the heart of the Chestnut Tree. A little breeze was shaking its new green leaves, and the same breeze, whistling through the window frames, was making the pendants of the chandelier shiver and sway till they chimed together like tiny bells.

Curiosity listened to the music for a moment. Then, turning away to find somewhere to hide, she squeaked with shock as she came face to face with another Mouse. The Mouse was very thin and rather pale. And it looked as alarmed as Curiosity felt.

'Aimée!' she cried. 'You've been very quick!'

'Been very quick,' agreed the Mouse.

They leaned towards each other and Curiosity saw that between the other Mouse's eyes, there was a tuft of snow-white fur.

'Oh!' she said with a shaky laugh. 'So that's it! Hello ME!'

The Mirror, where her other self had appeared, stretched the whole width of the mantel shelf and reached right up to the ceiling. It was freckled with brown stains and speckled with sparks of sunlight reflected off the swinging chandelier. It reminded Curiosity of the Mirror in her Parlour under the seventh stair and she was so pleased to

meet her-
self again that
she started to twizzle.
It was a long time since she had
twizzled and at first she turned
very slowly. But gradually she
built up speed until she and her
other self were whirling giddily among the dancing flecks of light. She had almost reached the
point of stillness at the heart of her spin when,
mingled with the music of the chandelier, she
heard a merry, tinkling laugh.

Curiosity stopped so suddenly that her leg

buckled under her and she sat down with a bump. When the room settled down around her she saw Aimée perched on the edge of the mantel shelf. She was rocking to and fro and clapping her paws.

'How d'you do that?' she cried. 'Teach me how to do it!'

Curiosity had never heard Aimée laugh before. She did not want to spoil it by explaining that twizzling was not something a Mouse could simply learn.

'I suppose I could try,' she began. 'But...'

She did not have time to finish the sentence before, in a flurry of tail and whiskers, in a scurry of squeaks and squeals, Aimée fled away from her along the shelf and vanished beneath the tapestry.

'*Now* what did I say?' wondered Curiosity.

Standing up, she went to the edge of the mantel shelf and looked about her. And there, crouching on the ledge outside the middle window, she saw Ethelred. His orange fur flamed in the sun. His eyes smouldered with green fire.

'You!' he snarled, looking directly back at her. 'I'm going to get YOU...'

And striking out with one paw he dragged his

claws down the glass until it screeched as if in pain.

'S-SOON,' he hissed. 'VERY S-SOON. Jus-st you wait and S-SEE!'

CHAPTER ELEVEN

From then on, Ethelred spent all his time prowling the garden outside the Drawing Room and growling out threats. Or he would lie for hours on the window sill, glowering in at them as Curiosity tried to teach Aimée how to twizzle.

Aimée was changing. The more time she spent with Curiosity the more cheerful and lively she became. Although she could not even stand on one hind leg, let alone turn on it, she would not give up trying. And she began to ask questions about the World beyond The Manor. She asked almost as many questions as Curiosity did.

Bertrand and Ralph, on the other hand, grew gloomier and moodier than ever.

'It's you ze Cat want,' moaned Ralph, scowling at Curiosity from under the sofa. 'Wiz your comings and your goings, your twiddlings and your nosy-parkering, you drive 'im into a frenzy!'

Curiosity tossed her head and flounced away. But she was beginning to feel that her Quest had brought her to a dead end. Although there was still a lot of The Manor she had not yet investigated, Ethelred was now making it impossible. Trapped, like the de Souris, in the Drawing Room, she found herself thinking more and more often of the Jones's house. She wondered how Great-Great-Grandfather Serendipity was, and what Uncle Serenity was doing. She missed Dimity and Alacrity. Occasionally she even missed Uppity...

The trouble was, she did not want to leave Aimée.

'What's the matter?' asked Aimée. 'You haven't asked a question for ages and you look all sad!'

'I was thinking,' sighed Curiosity. 'About home...'

For a moment Aimée was quiet and then she said, 'If you go back – can I come with you?'

Curiosity stared at her in surprise.

'Won't you be scared?' she said. 'You've never even been Outside!'

Aimée rose on her two hind legs and tottered in a clumsy circle.

'But I am so bored 'ere!' she said, mimicking Ralph.

'I want to see ze World!'

'What about your brothers?'

'What about them?' asked Aimée, flopping back on to all fours.

Curiosity giggled.

'I suppose they wouldn't miss us much!' she said.

'Exactement!' said Aimée.

Later that day Aimée told Bertrand and Ralph what she was going to do.

'Mon Dieu!' said Ralph. 'You will never get out of zis 'ouse alive! Ze Cat will make mousemeat out of you!'

'*Mincemeat*, dear boy,' said Bertrand.

They made a half-hearted attempt to persuade their sister to stay but Curiosity could tell that they were both really glad to be rid of *her*.

'We'll be leaving at sunset,' she said. 'When Ethelred goes in for his supper.'

The thought of supper made her tummy ache. She had eaten nothing since the night before and then all she had found were two mouldy crumbs of bread.

The Cat, as usual, was stretched out on the window ledge and looking up she saw the slow rise and fall of his ribs. The sun glistened on his

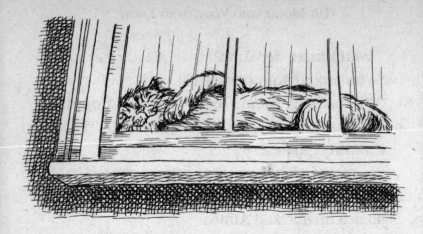

whiskers but his terrible eyes were fast shut.

'Ethelred's *asleep*,' she said to Aimée. 'Why don't we go to forage *now?*'

Aimée quivered uncertainly. She was more used to being hungry than Curiosity was.

'If you're coming with me on a Quest,' said Curiosity slyly, 'shouldn't you start to practise being brave?'

So Aimée followed her through the gap in the floorboards and along the track that led to the West Wing. The track did not go all the way into the kitchen but ended in a Mousehole in the corridor outside. Telling Aimée to stay where she was, Curiosity dropped out of the Mousehole and on to the stone floor.

From inside the kichen

she could hear the People's voices and seeping out through the crack under the door was Ethelred's fishy scent. But it was old and faint and there was no other sign of the Cat. Sniffing the air, she waited a moment. The tantalising smell of frying bacon drifted towards her and, keeping close to the skirting board, she crept nearer to the kitchen.

Still she could detect no danger and she was just wondering whether to call Aimée to join her, when she heard one of the People give a loud shriek and the door burst open.

The door struck Curiosity and flung her back against the wall. As she staggered about, dazed, she saw Ethelred come dashing through with a rasher of bacon dangling from his jaws. There was another shriek, and flying out after him came a dish-cloth and a wooden spoon. Then the door banged shut.

Ethelred stopped right beside the Mousehole.

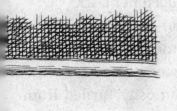

Hunching over the bacon, he tore at it with his strong teeth. Curiosity tried to shuffle backwards to hide herself in the shadowy corner between the doorpost

a n d
the wall.
But Ethelred's
keen ears heard her movement
and he raised his head.

Mustn't look into his eyes, thought Curiosity, trembling from head to tail. Mustn't let him *mesmerize!*

With a great effort she turned away from him but the Cat's green glare dragged her back.

'Aaaarrr,' he growled. 'At la-ast!'

As he advanced on her Ethelred seemed to fill the narrow corridor. There was nowhere to run, no way to escape. Again Curiosity turned from his stare. And again. The growl in the Cat's throat deepened to a roar and the fur on his neck stood out in a bristling ruff. Her turns quickened and from many moons of practice she found herself rising on her hind legs.

Ethelred's head jerked back and his jaws opened wide. He was now so close that as she spun once more to face him, she could see the shreds of meat still clinging to his fangs. Her right leg lifted and she twirled smoothly on her left. Faster she went, and faster. She had never twizzled so hard in all her life.

The Cat dissolved into a fiery blur and his eyes were no more than a green smear in the gloom of the corridor. From somewhere – she could not tell where – Curiosity heard a yowling sound that seemed to ebb and flow to her turnings. Then, through the whisk and whirr of the air around her, she saw Ethelred himself rear up.

Lurching from side to side as though he were strung on the end of a swinging rope, Ethelred too began to revolve. Wider he swung and more wildly until his orange fur seemed to blaze and crackle while his yowl thinned out to a shrill whine.

And just as Curiosity felt her strength give out and her leg crumple beneath her, the Cat uttered

one last shuddering howl and sank in a heap on the stones of the floor.

CHAPTER TWELVE

When, after many adventures, Curiosity at last came back to the Jones's house, it was almost summer. The apple tree outside the back door was a froth of pink and white blossom and only that morning the first Swallow had returned to its nesting place under the eaves.

On the doorstep Uncle Serenity was grooming himself in the sun when he saw a small, dark shadow twizzling towards him through the drifts of petals that lay in the yard.

'Bon jour, Uncle,' said the shadow as it twirled to a stop at the foot of the step.

'Whatever are you doing out here in broad daylight? Where's Mrs Jones? Has she taken the Dog for his walk? Is Mr Jones about? What's happening?'

Uncle Serenity looked closely at the slim brown Mouse with the tuft of white fur between her eyes.

'If you weren't as skinny as a piece of string,' he said, 'and didn't have such a Frenchified air about you, I'd swear you were my niece Curiosity!'

Curiosity laughed. Through the open door she could smell bread baking and the rich dark fragrance of Mrs Jones's chocolate cake. As Uncle Serenity sloped off into the larder, she beckoned to Aimée who was waiting shyly in the shadows beneath the tree.

Together they scuttled across the floor to forage under the table where the best tit-bits were always to be found. While Curiosity munched a morsel of chocolate cake, Aimée looked about her in astonishment. She had never seen so much food. She picked at a knob of bread and then pattered across the room to the stove where the kettle was singing a welcoming sort of song.

The Parrot stuck her head through the bars of her cage and fixed one golden eye on Aimée.

'Scupper me!' she squawked. 'What have we here! A Mermouse?' And cackling with laughter she bobbed up and down until the cage rattled.

Curiosity had told Aimée all about the Parrot so she took no notice but carried on eating a crumb of Stilton cheese she had just found. As she nibbled she caught the quiet murmur of mouse voices from behind the stove.

'Who's that talking?' she asked as Curiosity came over to join her.

'I expect it's Grandad,' said Curiosity, 'and some of my cousins. Let's go and see.'

With Aimée following her she slipped through a gap between the skirting board and the wall and scampered along the track to Great-Great-Grandfather Serendipity's Parlour. And there, as she had guessed, they found Uppity, Dimity, Homity and Alacrity all listening to a story.

'Hi, everybody!' cried Curiosity. 'Regardez-moi! Look at me! I'm back! And see who I've brought with me!'

At once Great-Great-Grandfather stopped talking and the four up-and-coming young Mice turned round.

'Oh boring!' groaned Uppity. 'If it isn't Wonder Mouse!'

'Wander Mouse is more like it!' cried Alacrity in delight. 'I thought you'd gone for ever, Curiosity!'

'My dear Curiosity,' exclaimed Serendipity. 'How very nice to see you again. And who is your little friend?'

Aimée thought Great-Great-Grandfather had a kind, wise face and although she was shy she did not feel afraid.

'Please, Monsieur,' she said. 'My name is Aimée.'

Dimity and Alacrity frisked around her, nudging her gently with their noses.

'What a lovely accent! What a pretty name!' they cried. 'And how silky your whiskers are!'

Then, after arguing about who should sit next to her, they all settled down again in a circle and insisted that Curiosity should tell them everything about her Quest.

'Oh dear,' whispered Homity when she came to the end of her tale. 'I'm glad I'm not a wanting-to-know sort of Mouse. Wanting to know led Curiosity into such dreadful DANGER!'

'My dear Child,' said Great-Great-Grandfather, who could not for the moment remember Homity's name. 'There can never be a true Quest without Danger. What's more, although Curiosity did not find the answers to all her questions, she did, nevertheless, learn a great deal...'

'I learned some French,' agreed Curiosity. 'And a bit of History...'

'Most importantly of all, however,' continued Serendipity, 'she has brought GREAT HONOUR to the Tribe of Mousity...'

He paused to scratch his left ear where the tip was missing. Long ago, when he himself was young and brave, he had lost it in a battle with a Cat.

'In all my long life,' he marvelled, 'I have never heard of a Mouse who defeated a CAT!'

'Huh,' muttered Uppity.

Great-Great-Grandfather frowned and shook his paw at him.

'Curiosity's Quest,' he went on firmly, 'ended in a deed so VALIANT – and so amazing – that the very words "*Curiosity Killed the Cat*" will go down in our history. Will be for ever part of our language!'

Curiosity blinked and the end of her nose went rather pink.

'I don't think,' she began, 'that I actually k...'

But Serendipity raised his paw for silence. He had enjoyed making a speech but his old bones ached from sitting still for so long and he felt suddenly very tired. Standing up he patted Curiosity on the head and then shuffled away to lie down on his couch of red velvet.

'Should I say... I mean, ought I to tell them... about Ethelred?' Curiosity whispered to Aimée. But Aimée only shook her head and laughed her tinkling laugh.

Serendipity's grey head sank slowly on to his paws and he began to snore.

'He's fallen asleep,' cried Alacrity, jumping up. 'Quick, quick! Let's all go and play Mouse-and-Cat!'

After their long journey, however, Curiosity and Aimée were also very tired. So leaving the others they climbed the track to the space under the seventh stair.

Curiosity's Parlour was exactly the same as when she had left it. There in the corner was the fragment of mirror. There was the sunlight dancing in it. And there, coming to meet them with a pleased expression, was Curiosity's other self – with another Mouse beside her.

'I'm glad I went on my Quest,' said Curiosity, doing a happy little twizzle. 'And it *didn't* come to a dead end, did it? Because although I didn't actually *kill* the Cat, I don't think Ethelred will ever trouble your brothers – or any other Mouse – again!'

'Exactement,' giggled Aimée, remembering

how Curiosity's twizzling had mesmerized Ethelred, and how, after the Cat had twizzled *himself* into a fit, he had slunk away from The Manor with his tail between his legs.

'But best of all,' said Curiosity, as she slowed down and came face to face with Aimée, 'I found a FRIEND!'

Aimée was so overcome that she jiggled up and down on the spot. She had never *quite* learned how to twizzle.

'I think the Jones's house is *wonderful*,' she said, when she could speak again.

'Me too,' agreed Curiosity, curling herself up in the sun. 'But Grandad was right. The World *is* a Most Marvellous place. And although it's good to be home there's still so much I want to know. I wonder, Aimée... I mean... what if *sometime*... when you're ready, you know... you and I set off together on *another* Quest?'

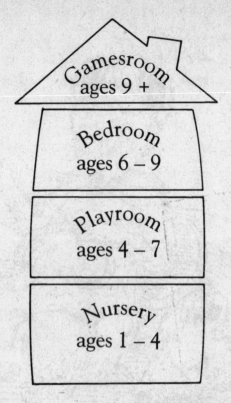

Gamesroom
ages 9 +

Bedroom
ages 6 – 9

Playroom
ages 4 – 7

Nursery
ages 1 – 4

Our Bloomsbury Book House has a special room for
each age group – this one is from the Bedroom.

Watch out for more MOUSE TALES by Anne Merrick:
A Message From a Mouse   0 7475 2614 1 PB 0 7475 2640 0 HB
The Castaway Mouse   0 7475 2659 1 PB 0 7475 2660 5 HB
A Mouse in Winter   0 7475 2661 3 PB 0 7475 2662 1 HB